LIBRARIANS

A TO Z

Text and Photographs
Jean Johnson

Walker and Company
New York, New York

Acknowledgements

Many librarians assisted me with the text and photos in this book. I would like to thank the librarians at the following Charlotte, N.C., libraries: Public Library of Charlotte & Mecklenburg County, Central Piedmont Community College Library, University of North Carolina at Charlotte, Queens College, Charlotte Country Day School Library, Devonshire and Dilworth Elementary School Libraries and Presbyterian Hospital Learning Resource Center. Librarians at the York County Public Library in Rock Hill, S.C., and the Gaston County Public Library in Gastonia, N.C., also provided invaluable assistance. A special thanks to Pat Siegfried, head of Children's Services at the Public Library of Charlotte & Mecklenburg County, for her support and encouragement.

First published in the United States of America in 1988 by the Walker Publishing Company, Inc.

Published simultaneously in Canada by Thomas Allen & Son Canada, Limited, Markham, Ontario.

Library of Congress Cataloging-in-Publication Data

Johnson, Jean, 1943-
    Librarians A to Z/text and photographs, Jean Johnson.
      p.   cm.—(Community helpers series)
    Summary: The letters of the alphabet introduce aspects of the work of librarians, including art, desks, exhibits, files, and glue.
    ISBN 0-8027-6841-5. ISBN 0-8027-6842-3 (lib. bdg.)
    1. Librarians—Juvenile literature. 2. Libraries—Juvenile literature. [1. Librarians. 2. Libraries. 3. Alphabet.]
    I. Title. II. Series: Community helpers series (New York, N.Y.) Z682.J6 1988
[E]—dc19   88-21441
                                                         CIP
                                                          AC

Printed in the United States of America

10 9 8 7 6 5 4 3 2 1

Book design by Laurie McBarnette

For all librarians

Other Titles in the Community Helpers Series

A Art

This librarian is helping children with an art project. First, she read them a story about pinwheels. Now she is showing them how to make their own pinwheels.

B

Books

Librarians buy books for libraries. They read magazines and newspapers that tell about new books. Then they order the books their libraries need. When the books come, librarians and their helpers unpack the boxes. They like seeing all the new books.

C Cataloger

This librarian is a cataloger. Using a computer program, she catalogs books by giving each new book a number. Then she describes the book. This information is put onto cards. The cards are put into drawers in the card catalog. Some libraries use computer catalogs instead of card catalogs.

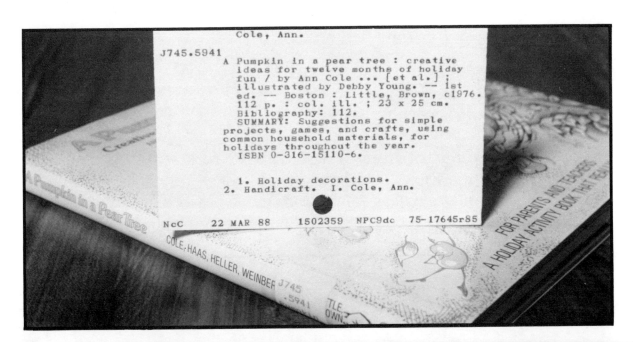

```
                    Cole, Ann.

J745.5941       A Pumpkin in a pear tree : creative
                ideas for twelve months of holiday
                fun / by Ann Cole ... [et al.] ;
                illustrated by Debby Young. -- 1st
                ed. -- Boston : Little, Brown, c1976.
                112 p. : col. ill. ; 23 x 25 cm.
                Bibliography: 112.
                SUMMARY: Suggestions for simple
                projects, games, and crafts, using
                common household materials, for
                holidays throughout the year.
                ISBN 0-316-15110-6.

                1. Holiday decorations.
                2. Handicraft.  I. Cole, Ann.

NcC       22 MAR 88       1502359   NPC9dc   75-17645r85
```

D Desks

Librarians work at different kinds of desks. Some work at the check-out desk. They answer questions and help people check out books. Some librarians work at an office desk in a workroom. They order new books, catalog them, and get the books ready to be put onto the shelves.

E

Exhibits

These librarians are setting up an exhibit of dinosaur books so that people will want to read about dinosaurs. Librarians set up many different kinds of exhibits.

F Files

This librarian is helping a child look in the files for animal pictures. Files help to organize pictures, maps, and booklets and keep them neat.

G
Glue

Librarians use white glue to stick card pockets and date-due slips into books. They also use glue to mend torn pages and repair books.

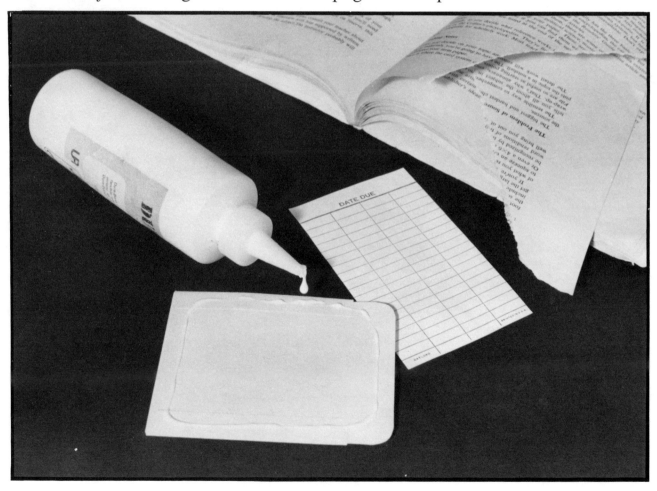

H Helpers

These library helpers are getting paperback books ready to put onto the shelves. Many workers help in the library. Some helpers are paid, and others volunteer to work without pay.

Ink pad and stamps

Librarians use ink pads and many different kinds of stamps. The stamps are kept on a rack called a tree. A property stamp marks the name of the library on each new book. The date-due stamp tells when a book must be returned.

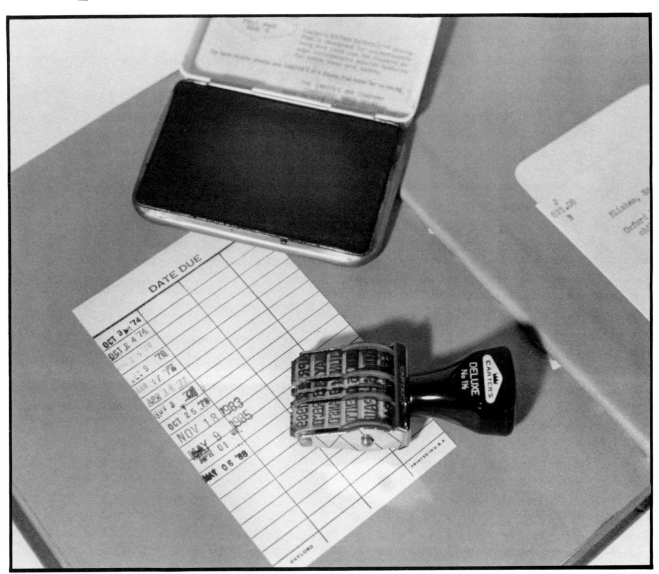

J Jackets

Paper jackets protect books. The librarian and her helper are covering a book jacket with plastic so it won't rip or get dirty.

K

Kickstool

Librarians use kickstools to reach books on high shelves. They sit on them to look on low shelves. Kickstools are easy to push across the floor. People who come to the library may use the kickstools, too.

L Librarians

There are different kinds of librarians. This school librarian is teaching children to find books. She also tells stories, shows films, and buys books and equipment for the library.

This medical librarian works in a hospital library. She has books, models, and materials to help doctors, nurses, and others who work at the hospital. Other librarians work in college, government, public, and special libraries. Special libraries can be devoted to law, business, museums, etc.

M Magazines

This librarian is in charge of magazines at her library. She orders magazines for children and for adults. She displays new magazines, and she stores the old ones under the shelf or in a back room.

N

Newspapers

Librarians order newspapers from many places. Each day new editions are put out so people can read news about other cities and countries. The old papers are stored in the back of the library or kept on microfilm.

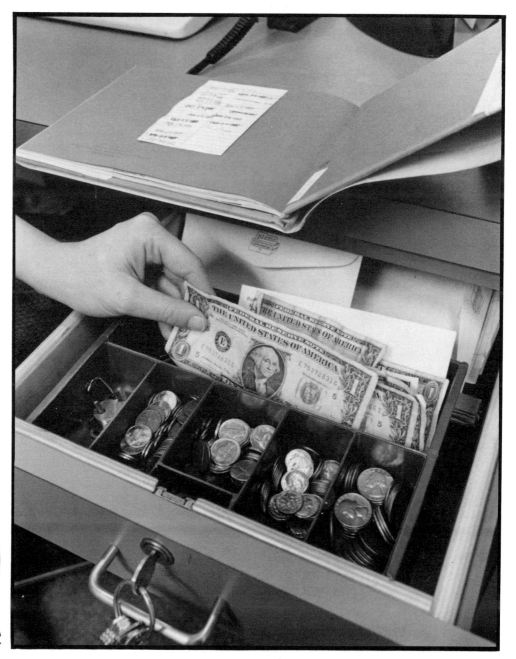

O
Overdue

If library books are not returned on time, they are overdue. Some librarians charge money for overdue books. They often buy new books with the money they collect.

P

Programs

These children are watching a library program about African dances and songs. Librarians plan programs that make us want to learn about our world and read books.

 Questions

This boy and his father have come to the library to ask a question about soccer. The librarians at this desk are called reference librarians, and they answer questions on many subjects. They use special books, telephones, and computers to find answers to questions.

R
Recordings

Librarians buy and catalog recordings of music, stories, and foreign languages. The recordings are records, tapes, or compact discs. They also buy listening equipment and make sure it works well.

S Storyteller

Some librarians are storytellers. They are specially trained to read or tell stories to children. When the storytelling is finished, the children like to look at the books.

T Traveling librarians

This traveling librarian drives a mini-library called a bookmobile. She takes books to people who do not live near a library. People walk or drive to the bookmobile stop. They borrow books and return them when the bookmobile comes back. If people are sick or handicapped, the librarian takes books to their homes.

U

Unusual

Some librarians have unusual things for people to check out. This boy is checking out a computer to take home. Other librarians have small animals in cages to check out. Toys, cameras, and even fishing rods can be borrowed from some libraries.

Videos and films

This librarian buys videos and films for the library. She views the videos or films so she can catalog them. Librarians also buy TV sets and projectors to show the videos and films.

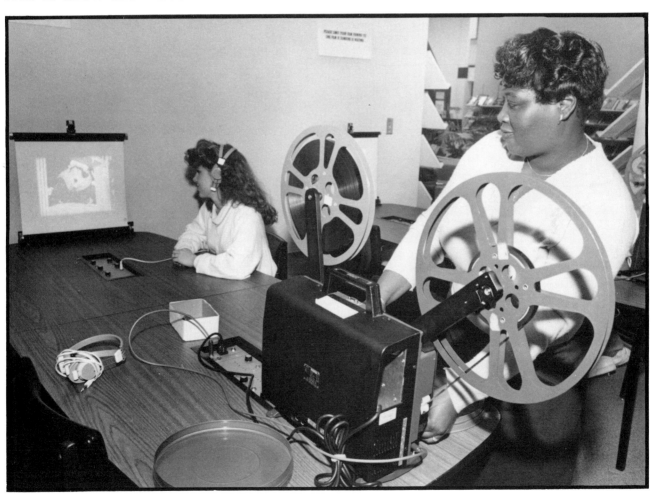

W
Weeding

Librarians are always weeding out (discarding) books that are not useful or that are badly damaged. The books might be sold at a library book sale.

 X

Some librarians use an *X* to mark weeded books. The library does not need these books anymore. The *X* shows that the books no longer belong on the library shelves.

Your library

Your library may be small, large, old, or new. Libraries differ, but they all have librarians to help you find books, magazines, videos, or whatever you need.

Z Zigzag

A zigzag book is a folding book. This librarian is showing a very old Japanese zigzag book. Special and very old books like this are kept in a rare book room. The librarian takes good care of rare books so people can enjoy them for a long time.

More About Librarians

In this section the work of librarians is further described in words and pictures to bring about discussion and a greater awareness of the many roles librarians play in helping get people in our communities.

Librarians play an important role in our communities. They provide library books and materials that help people to learn more about themselves, their society, and the world. Librarians enjoy helping people, are informed about current events, and keep up with new trends in technology. Professional librarians go to school for advanced degrees in library or information science.

There are many different careers within the library profession. The type of job a librarian has depends upon the size of the library and the kind of community it serves. In large libraries, librarians specialize and work in one department, such as collection development, technical services, public service, or administration. In small libraries, librarians work at many different jobs. Many librarians are employed by special libraries that serve professional people such as lawyers, engineers, physicians, and scientists. There are also school, university, government, and public libraries.

Librarians who work in public service are responsible for reference services, programs for children, young adults, and adults, community outreach activities, bibliographic lists and instruction, and circulation of books and materials.

All libraries offer reference services. Large libraries have a special desk for reference librarians, who are trained to answer your questions by using reference books, microfilm, microfiche, computers, and the telephone. They may also take requests for interlibrary loans and refer library users to additional materials at other libraries. Reference work can be demanding, so these librarians usually work three- or four-hour shifts and then move to a desk in the workroom where they may select books or do research on reference questions.

Children's librarians work in public or school libraries. One of their most important jobs is helping you find good books. They also plan creative programs to promote reading. These include storytelling, films, art activities, and puppet shows. These librarians show children and young adults how to use the library and find materials for homework assignments. School librarians teach library science skills beginning in the second or third grades. They are often called media specialists because they take care of so many school resources.

Librarians who work in collection development select new books and resource materials. They decide what to buy after they study preview copies of books, recommendations about books, and book reviews. In university, government, and large public libraries, librarians specialize, often buying materials only for one area, such as history or sports. Librarians in collection development also decide which books and materials are out-of-date, damaged beyond repair, or useless to the collection. Discarded books are often sold at library book sales. Weeding is an important job.

Librarians in technical services order, catalog, and process books and materials after they are selected by the librarians in collection development. Those who order books are called acquisition librarians. In a small library, the acquisition librarian both selects and orders the books, acting as a combination of collection development and technical services librarian. Librarians who are catalogers provide information and organize books so that similar subjects stand together on the shelves. Purchasing audio-visual materials, maps, documents, photographs, and other library materials is also part of technical services. After cataloging, books and materials are sent to processing, where they are labeled with a number and prepared for circulation. Magazines and newspapers are checked off on a file as they arrive. Back issues are bound together or saved on microfilm (rolls of film) or microfiche (sheets of film).

In large public libraries, librarians may operate a bookmobile or travel in their cars to set up book collections in nursing homes, day care centers, prisons, or centers for the handicapped. They may also bring magazines, large print, and braille books. Many of these librarians show films and present book programs.

A librarian in administration may direct the entire staff of a library or one department within a large library. Small independent or branch libraries are usually managed by one librarian and several assistants. Administrative librarians also work with people in finance, public relations, support services, and personnel who may or may not be librarians.

Computers have made significant changes in many librarians' jobs. They simplify book orders, print catalog cards, make book labels, and eliminate the tedious job of filing catalog cards. Many catalogers use a computer data base to get a description of a book and its call number. Some libraries store bibliographic information in a computer instead of in a card catalog. You would use a computer terminal to look up books. Computers store circulation information and many libraries use them at the checkout desk. Special libraries use computer programs and daily or weekly news services to provide them with up-to-date information.

Librarians perform a variety of services and work in many different kinds of libraries. They help people understand the past and make intelligent decisions about the future. They are one of our communities' greatest resources.